The warm-up

For Françoise who said, "Why don't you
do a book about football called Goal!?"
And I said, "Hmm…"

This edition produced for The Book People Ltd, Hall Wood Avenue, Haydock, St Helens WAll 9UL
First published in hardback in Great Britain by Andersen Press Ltd in 1997
First published in paperback by Picture Lions in 1999
This edition published by Collins Picture Books in 2002

1 3 5 7 9 10 8 6 4 2
ISBN: 0 00 770806 8

Picture Lions and Collins Picture Books are imprints of the Children's Division, part of HarperCollins Publishers Ltd.
Text and illustrations copyright © Colin McNaughton 1997
The author/illustrator asserts the moral right to be identified as the author/illustrator of the work.
A CIP catalogue record for this title is available from the British Library.

The HarperCollins website address is: www.fireandwater.com

Manufactured in Thailand for Imago

Colin McNaughton

GOAL!

TED SMART

Preston is playing football
in the garden one day

when his mum asks him
to go to the shop. Preston
decides to take his ball

and Preston, the world's most brilliant footballer, sets off.

He beats one player, then
another, goes round the
goalkeeper and shoots…

And the fans go wild:
"Ooh-ah-Preston Pig.
I said ooh-ah-Preston Pig!"

And Preston has the ball once more. He runs the whole length of the park and shoots…

It's a goal!

And the huge crowd chants:
"Preston, Preston,
He's the best 'un!"

And Preston goes looking
for his hat-trick.

And this is incredible!
He's off on another run!
He goes round one. He goes
round two, three and he shoots…

Let me at him!

It's a
goal!

That makes it three goals to nil,

but 'Super Preston' isn't finished yet!

He dribbles past the
great Giggs, swerves past
the magical Owen,

sweeps past Shearer,
puts the ball through the
legs of Beckham and shoots…

It's a goal!

Four-goal Preston sets off
home with the bread.

Mister Wolf leaves
the supermarket.

Mister Wolf takes a short cut
and lies in wait for Preston.

And Mister Wolf
gobbles Preston up.

Well, not really,
but that was his plan.

Extra time

Collect all the Preston Pig Stories

0-00-714013-4

0-00-714011-8

0-00-714014-2

0-00-714015-0

0-00-664715-4

0-00-714012-6

0-00-712635-2

0-00-713235-2

0-00-713236-0

0-00-713234-4

0-00-713237-9

0-00-712371-X

0-00-712370-1

0-00-712372-8

Colin McNaughton is one of Britain's most highly-acclaimed picture book talents and a winner of many prestigious awards. His Preston Pig Stories are hugely successful with Preston now starring in his own animated television series on CITV.